A Random House book
Published by Random House Australia Pty Ltd
Level 3, 100 Pacific Highway, North Sydney NSW 2060
www.randomhouse.com.au

 Penguin
Random House
Australia

First published by Random House Australia in 2016

Addresses for the Penguin Random House group of companies can be found at
global.penguinrandomhouse.com/offices

National Library of Australia
Cataloguing-in-Publication entry

Creator: Darlison, Aleesah, author
Title: Aim for the top / Aleesah Darlison; illustrator Cat MacInnes
ISBN: 9780143781141 (pbk)
Series: Netball gems; 5
Target Audience: For primary school age
Subjects: Netball – Juvenile fiction
         Netball players – Juvenile fiction
Dewey Number: A823.4

Cover illustration by Cat MacInnes
Cover design by Kirby Armstrong
Typeset in 15/20.7 pt Adobe Garamond by Midland Typesetters, Australia
Printed in Australia by Griffin Press, an accredited ISO AS/NZS 14001:2004 Environmental Management System printer

Penguin Random House Australia uses papers that are natural, renewable and recyclable products and made from wood grown in sustainable forests. The logging and manufacturing processes are expected to conform to the environmental regulations of the country of origin.

NETBALL GEMS

Aim for the Top

Written by
A. DARLISON

Illustrated by
CAT MACINNES

RANDOM HOUSE AUSTRALIA

Chapter One

Jade's palms were sweaty and butterflies whirled around in her stomach. She always felt nervous before a game. Winning was everything; that's what her dad always said.

'Aim for the top,' he would say. 'Winning is what matters.'

Today, winning was more important than ever. The Under 13s Marrang Gems were playing their first ever semifinal!

Their game was against Thomson, the team that placed first in the comp. Although the Gems had defeated Thomson before, the Thomson players regularly thrashed each team they were up against. The Gems had to win their game today to secure their place in the grand final. If they lost, they would have to compete in a play-off and might get knocked out of the competition altogether.

Jade gazed out the car window as Mum drove to the netball courts. She imagined her team winning the grand final to become the Under 13s champions.

How awesome would that be!

'Jade, stop tapping your foot.' Mum interrupted her thoughts.

'Sorry.'

To distract herself, Jade carefully retied her rainbow-coloured shoelaces. She'd bought them especially for this game. She hoped they would bring her good luck.

Jade's pre-game shoelace routine was the same every Saturday. She had to retie her laces exactly three times each. Neat ties that were double-knots.

Jade had learnt the importance of a pre-game routine from her dad. Jade's dad, Casper, was sports-mad. So was Jade's mum, Olive. They owned an elite sports training centre. When they weren't running boot camps or kickboxing sessions, they were competing in marathons.

Sports and fitness were everything to the Mathison family.

'Have you got your water bottle?' Jade's mum asked.

'All filled and ready to go.'

After a pause, her mum went on. 'You know Dad would be here if he could, don't you?'

'Sure.' Jade nodded.

She knew her dad loved her, but he rarely watched her games even though she'd been playing a long time, ever since she'd started out in NetSetGO. If Dad wasn't working or running marathons, he was usually with Jade's older brother Jet. Jet was a junior rugby star. He played for the Under 16s Marrang Falcons. He also played for regional and state teams and often competed in rugby carnivals.

'Maybe Dad can come next week if you play.'

Hmmm, Jade thought. *I wouldn't count on it.*

Mum pulled up at the netball courts and turned the engine off. 'Time to hop out.'

Jade clambered out and slung her sports bag over her shoulder. She poked her head through the car window. 'Well, at least you're watching me today. Come on, Mum, or I'll miss the warm up.'

Mum's face fell. 'Oh, darling, I'm sorry. Didn't I mention it? I must have forgotten in the rush this morning.'

'Mention what?' Jade said.

'That I can't stay today. Mr Marks has a physio session at the centre so I have to go in. He's in terrible pain.'

Jade bit her lip so she wouldn't cry. She knew her parents had to work but today was special. It was her first ever semifinal.

Mum started the car again. 'I really am sorry, Jade. But think of poor Mr Marks.'

Think of poor me, Jade thought.

'Jade! Come on!'

Jade turned and saw her coach, Janet, carrying her huge sports bag onto the court.

'Okay, Mum,' Jade said. 'See you later.'

'Can you walk home after the game?' Mum said. 'I'm not sure I'll be finished before you're done.'

Jade nodded. 'Sure.'

'Good luck, Jadey, I hope you win,' Mum called as she drove off.

My day had better improve, Jade thought. *This is a terrible start.*

Chapter Two

Jade dropped her bag on the sideline and jogged over to the other girls. Everyone was there: Maddy, Phoebe, Prani, Lily, Sienna, Isabella and the new girl, Maia.

If we win today, maybe Dad will come next week, Jade thought.

'Nice shoelaces.' Maia pointed to Jade's rainbow-coloured laces.

Jade vaguely heard Maia but she wasn't really paying attention. She was too upset. All she wanted to do was cry.

From the corner of her eye, she saw Maia whisper to Maddy.

Is she talking about me? Jade wondered. *Why can't she just leave me alone? At least her parents are here watching.*

It made Jade cross to think her teammates might be talking about her. And it made her even more cross because it made her remember that feeling she always had of never quite belonging in the Gems. She often felt left out. Most of the Gems went to the same school and Jade could see that they shared a close bond. Isabella was the only girl from the Gems who went to Jade's school but they were in different classes and never spent time together. Besides, since Maia had joined the team, Isabella seemed to spend all her spare time with her.

'Hey, everyone,' said Sienna. 'Why did the chicken cross the road?'

Jade lifted an eyebrow. 'To get to the other side?'

'No, silly. She wanted to stretch her legs.'

In a fit of giggles, Sienna tucked her hands in her armpits, flapping and squawking like a chicken. Prani joined in, clucking and flapping her wings too.

Sienna definitely had the best sense of humour in the group. She was always playing pranks. And Prani was always laughing and seemed to like having fun, too. But sometimes their silliness could be distracting.

Jade noticed that Maddy had wandered off by herself, cradling a netball in her arms and staring into space.

Don't tell me Maddy's daydreaming, now! Why can't any of them focus? Don't they want to win?

'Okay, girls.' Janet trotted over carrying several netballs, which she placed at her feet.

'Enough antics. This is a big game for us. Our first semifinal!'

Everyone except Jade cheered.

'Congratulations on making it this far,' Janet continued. 'You've done amazingly well in your first year as a team.' She briefly studied each girl in turn. 'Today's game against Thomson will be tough. You'll have to dig deep and play hard. Because it's such an important game today, I thought we'd squeeze in some extra practice, so thanks for coming down earlier than usual. Let's start with passing drills.'

Janet often made the Gems practise their ball skills because fast and accurate passing was crucial to the game.

'Chest passes first.' Janet tossed four balls out to four girls. 'Form pairs. Twenty chest passes each. Then bounce passes. Then high lob passes.'

Prani claimed Maddy as her partner by lightly donking her on the head with the ball. Sienna skipped over to Lily and bowed deeply, presenting her with a ball as if it were a precious jewel. At the same time, Isabella did a ballerina twirl before offering her ball to Maia. 'Please say you'll be my partner, Maia!'

While all this was going on, Jade and Phoebe stood watching.

Is it my imagination or does Phoebe look disappointed at being left to pair with me? wondered Jade. She gave a mental shrug. *Never mind. It doesn't bother me. I'm only here for the netball.*

When they had finished the first round of drills, Janet called out, 'Take two steps backwards and go through the drill again.'

Jade's anger and disappointment melted away. She began to enjoy the drill and forgot everything else. All that mattered was netball.

'I'm so good at this!' Jade said, loudly and super-confidently. 'Look at my perfect pass, Janet!' But as she threw the ball to Phoebe, she lost her balance. The netball flew over Phoebe's head and bounced away.

'Nobody's perfect, Jade,' Janet said. 'Keep trying.'

'It wasn't my fault,' Jade blurted out. She didn't like looking silly in front of her coach. 'Phoebe wasn't watching.'

Phoebe blushed. 'I was!'

The other girls stopped and stared.

Janet shook her head. 'We play as a team, Jade. We don't blame others. You need to think about that. And while you're doing that, you can keep the bench warm for the first quarter.'

'What?' Jade couldn't believe it. 'That's not fair.'

'I think it's very fair,' Janet said. 'Now, no more arguments. Go collect that ball. We're moving onto shooting drills.'

Chapter Three

Jade was not happy that she'd gone the entire first quarter without stepping on court.

I know I said the wrong thing, but what if Janet doesn't put me on in the second quarter? Jade worried.

She knew everyone had to take a turn on the bench. There were only seven players allowed on court at any time and the Gems had eight so the girls always took turns sitting out, just like they took turns rotating positions.

But the Gems were playing well. The score was 7–5 their way. It would be hard to justify switching positions when everything was going so well.

Jade peered at the score table to see the timer. Only two minutes left on the clock!

Phoebe, playing Goal Shooter, scored another goal with a fantastic shot from close range after Isabella, playing at Goal Attack, sent a bounce pass her way.

Goal Attack was Jade's favourite position and she was itching to be given a go at it today. Unlike the Goal Shooter, who was confined to the goal third, she loved that Goal Attack was able to move into the centre third and get involved in the action further up the court, while still being able to play in the goal third and score goals for the team.

The players returned to their starting positions. It was Marrang's turn for the centre pass so Prani, who was playing Centre, stepped into the circle.

The umpire's whistle sounded.

Prani passed to Maddy at Wing Attack, who had expertly jumped into the centre third as soon as the whistle had blown. Isabella called out for the ball from the far side of the court. Maddy threw a high lob pass over the head of the Thomson Wing Defence. It was a beautiful throw and Isabella trapped the ball in her hands perfectly. She pivoted, dodging her defender, and passed the ball to Prani, who had run up close to the goal circle.

When Phoebe called for the ball, Prani sent a bounce pass her way. But Phoebe was a long way from goal and her defender was directly in front of her.

Jade checked the timer. Fifteen seconds left!

'Shoot!' Jade shouted. 'The whistle is about to go!'

Phoebe moved her weight onto her right foot to take a side-step shot, which would help her move away from her defending player. But as she lifted her left foot off the ground, her right ankle buckled beneath her. Wincing in pain, Phoebe gathered herself to line up the shot.

Jade could see that Phoebe was biting her lip. *Has she hurt herself?* she wondered.

Phoebe released the ball, sending it upward with a flick of her wrist. Her left leg, still off the ground, was unsteady, causing her to wobble slightly. The ball struck the goal ring, rolled around the rim, then dropped out and dribbled over the baseline.

No goal.

Brrrp! The whistle sounded for the end of the quarter.

Phoebe had a pained look on her face as she hobbled towards the sideline. Her parents sat her on the bench.

'Are you okay?' Jade asked, keen to make up for her earlier mistake during their warm-up drills.

'I twisted my ankle,' Phoebe moaned. 'Ouch! It really hurts.'

'I'll get some ice,' Jade said. 'You stay put.'

'Thanks, Jade.' Phoebe's mum looked worried.

Jade rummaged through the first-aid kit for the icepack. When she brought it back, Phoebe put it straight on her ankle.

'Let's hope you haven't done any damage, Phoebe,' Janet said. 'I'm going to rest you and we'll see if the pain eases. Jade, you go on for her.' Janet handed her the Goal Shooter bibs. 'Everyone else stay in your positions.'

Goal Shooter wasn't Jade's favourite position, but she couldn't wait to shoot some goals.

'Come on, girls, let's win this game,' Jade said. 'No more errors.'

'What do you mean?' Maia asked. 'We played well that quarter.'

'Yes, but not well enough. Thomson can easily catch up if we don't play better. Winning is everything. *Especially* in a semifinal.'

Jade heard Prani mumble something that sounded like 'bossy', but before she could question her about it, the whistle blew warning the teams about the start of the second quarter.

'Enough chitchat,' Janet said. 'Time to go back on court.'

Chapter Four

'I'm free!' Isabella shouted. 'Pass it to me!'

Jade stood in the goal circle holding the netball. Although she was barely inside the line, she was confident she could shoot from where she was standing. Isabella was closer to the ring, but she wasn't as tall as Jade and often missed her shots.

I'm Goal Shooter, Jade thought. *I'm going to shoot this goal and we're going to win!*

The score was 8–8. From the start of the

second quarter, Thomson had made a strong comeback. Jade had scored one goal but missed a few others. Isabella had missed all of her attempts. The Gems needed to score.

Jade pretended to throw to Isabella. Her defender fell for the trick and moved away. Instead of passing the ball, however, Jade lifted it over her head and stepped forwards, raising her back foot as she did so. She then released the ball up towards the ring, flicking her wrist and pushing with her fingers.

The ball looped high into the air. It was lined up perfectly until a gust of wind drove it off course. The ball dropped over the ring and bounced into the goal circle where the Thomson Goal Keeper grabbed it. Before Jade knew it, Thomson had worked the ball down to their goal and had scored again.

Oh no. Jade's heart sank. *I messed up.*

'Never mind, it wasn't your fault,' Prani said. 'It was the wind.' She stuck her tongue out and crossed her eyes. 'See what it did to my face?'

Jade couldn't help laughing. Prani looked so silly!

'Thanks.'

'Any time!' Prani giggled.

Then the half-time whistle sounded and they trotted off court for a drink.

'Hang in there, Gems,' Janet said. 'We've still got half the game to get ahead. Try to focus on communicating better and trusting your teammates. The Goal Attack and Goal Shooter need to work as a team in the circle. If you're not in a position to shoot, pass it. Jade, Isabella was in a good position to shoot just then. You should have passed to her.'

'Okay,' Jade said.

Maybe Janet's right, Jade thought. *Then again, if it weren't for the wind, my shot probably would have gone in . . .*

'Good. We'll swap positions, now,' Janet said. 'Phoebe's ankle is still sore, so Isabella, you play Goal Shooter and Jade, you take Goal Attack.'

My favourite position! Jade thought joyfully.

Brrrp! The whistle blew and the girls went back on court.

But as hard as she tried, Jade couldn't get her shots at goal to go in. Neither could Isabella. By the end of the third quarter, the Gems were down 8–12.

Jade felt awful.

In the final quarter, Phoebe came back on as Goal Shooter while Prani volunteered to sit out and Maddy moved to Centre. The others held their positions.

The Gems rallied, closing the gap between Thomson and themselves so that the score was 11–12.

Two more goals to win. We can do this.

It was Maddy's turn for the centre pass. She

got the ball away to Lily, at Wing Attack, who sent a blistering chest pass straight to Jade.

Jade was well into the goal third, but not in the circle. She searched for support.

'Here!' Phoebe shouted from inside the circle.

Jade lobbed the ball over the defender to Phoebe then sprinted into the goal circle. 'Pass it back!'

Remembering what Janet had said about teamwork, Phoebe shot a short chest pass to Jade. Jade caught the ball then pivoted to face the goal. She was very close to the ring. Perhaps too close.

'Jade, here!' Phoebe called.

Ignoring her, Jade shot at goal. It missed. Again.

The final whistle sounded. The Gems had lost.

Oh boy did I mess up, Jade thought. *My terrible shooting cost us the game.*

Chapter Five

'Bad luck, girls,' Janet said, as they trudged off court. 'You should all be proud of your performances.'

But we lost, Jade thought.

'Great job, girls!' Parents crowded around, handing out oranges and water bottles and patting the girls on the back.

For the first time, Jade was glad her parents weren't there. She would have hated for her dad to see her lose.

'The good news is that you get another chance,' Janet said. 'This wasn't a knockout game so next week you play whoever wins today's other semifinal between the third- and fourth-placed teams. So I want you to go home and practise like you've never practised before. I'll see you on Wednesday for training.'

The girls said goodbye and wandered off with their parents.

Jade was left with Janet and Lily, who were packing up. Jade found a stray netball and carried it back to her coach.

'Thanks for helping out,' Janet said.

Jade was surprised. 'Aren't you angry at me for losing us the game?'

'Why would I be angry? Each of you did your best. All I want is for you girls to have fun and learn some netball skills. Whether we win or lose next week, you girls are all champions in my eyes.'

'But I missed so many goals.'

'We all have bad days.' Janet laughed. 'Don't be so hard on yourself. I meant what I said about you girls doing well in your first year as a team. I couldn't have asked for more as a coach. Or as a mum.' She hugged Lily, who beamed with pride.

'Really?' Jade said.

'Really. I've played a lot of netball,' Janet said, 'and if I had a dollar for every goal I'd missed, I'd be a wealthy woman indeed.'

'Were you a Goal Shooter like Phoebe?'

'Actually, my favourite position was Goal Attack,' Janet said.

Jade hadn't known that about Janet. None of the girls ever asked their coach about her days as a netball player. 'It's mine too.'

'I had noticed!' Janet joked.

'So tell me what I'm doing wrong,' Jade said.

'You need to trust your teammates and your Goal Shooter more,' Janet said. 'Your role as Goal Attack is to feed the ball to the Shooter so they can go for goal from close range. You have to be able to shoot from long range yourself, but ideally you need to get that netball to the Shooter.'

'Okay.' Jade nodded. 'I'll give it my best shot next time.'

Janet laughed.

Jade was confused. *Why is Janet laughing at me?* But then she realised what she'd said. 'Oh, I get it.' She grinned. 'Sorry, I didn't mean to make a joke.'

Janet rested her hand on Jade's shoulder. 'You know, it's okay to have fun with netball.' She glanced over at the carpark. 'Is your mum or dad late picking you up?'

Jade shook her head. 'Dad took Jet to rugby and Mum's at work. I'm walking home.'

'We'll give you a lift,' Janet said. 'We can stop for ice-cream on the way.'

'At that place on Mason Street that has the chocolate-dipped waffle cones?' Lily asked.

Janet nodded. 'That's the one.'

'I love that place!' Lily looped her arm through Jade's so they could walk together. 'My favourite flavour is caramel-choc crunch. What's yours?'

Jade looked down at Lily's arm looped through hers. Maybe it was the excitement of having ice-cream that made her do it. Either way, Jade was surprised at how much she liked it.

Chapter Six

'That was the best ice-cream ever,' Jade said, as she leant in the open passenger-side window of Janet's car. 'Thanks for taking me.'

'You're welcome. See you at training.'

'Bye, Jade!' Lily called as they drove off.

Using the key hidden beneath the geranium plant on the doorstep, Jade let herself in through the back door. The house was so quiet she could hear the clock above the fridge ticking.

Jade had never been good at making friends. Other girls at school hung out and had sleepovers. But not Jade.

She took her pink-and-white striped netball out of her bag. She loved how it felt in her hands. She tossed it up and caught it as she wandered into her bedroom, then she sat at her desk and switched the computer on. Balancing the netball on her knees, she googled Erin Bell.

Erin was Jade's favourite Diamonds player. She also played in the ANZ Championship for the Adelaide Thunderbirds. She was a fantastic Goal Attack and Goal Shooter. The motto on Erin's website was 'Aim, Shoot, Score!'

'I like that motto,' Jade said to the empty room. 'If only I played like Erin!'

Jade continued browsing through Erin's website and her profile on the Diamonds page, soaking up every bit of advice about playing netball that Erin had to give. One of the comments she liked most was about dreaming big and always doing everything in your control to make your dreams come true.

'My dream is to win the grand final in a few weeks,' Jade murmured to herself. 'And I'm sure going to do everything I can to make that dream come true!'

Moments later she heard voices at the front door. Relieved the others were finally home, Jade logged off her computer and rushed into the kitchen where Dad wrapped her in a bear hug.

'Guess what, Jadey?' he said.

'What?'

'Your brother scored two tries today. He won the game for the Falcons!' Dad was so excited he was shouting. 'My boy is a champion!'

'That's awesome,' Jade said.

Jet, who was 15 and already six feet tall, grinned. 'Thanks, sis. It's pretty embarrassing, though, when Dad gets excited on the sidelines. You can hear him cheering from across the other side of the field.'

I wish I had that problem.

'Jet's going to play for Australia one day,' Dad said. 'We're in the presence of a future Wallaby. Mark my words.'

Jet rolled his eyes. 'Whatever you reckon. I'm having a shower.'

'It's true!' Dad called after him. 'That's what happens when you aim for the top, son!' He turned to Jade. 'So how was netball?'

Jade hesitated, not wanting to disappoint him. 'Um . . . we lost.'

'Oh dear. What went wrong?'

Jade shrugged. 'Janet said we had a bad day.'

Dad moved about the kitchen, preparing dinner. He was a great cook and often made the family yummy meals. Jade sat down to tell him about the game, even though she was reluctant to admit how many shots she'd missed.

Dad nodded and said yes in all the right places, but he seemed distracted.

'We've got one more chance next week,' Jade said. 'Can you come and watch? It might be our last game.'

'Uh-huh,' Dad mumbled, as he marinated the steak.

'Really?! I can't wait!'

Dad jerked his head up when he heard the excitement in Jade's voice. Immediately she saw that he hadn't really been listening.

'Have you heard anything I've said?' Jade asked.

'Of course I have.'

'Well, what did I say?'

Dad pulled a funny face. He knew he'd been caught out. 'You need to work on your passing skills?'

'That's *so* not what I said.' Jade laughed, despite herself. She could never stay cross at Dad for long. 'I asked if you could watch me play next week.'

'I wish I could but I'm running the half-marathon and then I have an appointment with my tax accountant.'

'You're always busy.' Jade stood up, pouting. 'No one cares about netball.'

'Jadey, that's not true.' Dad washed his hands then rushed over to hug her. 'I wish I could get out of my meeting with the accountant but it's important for our business.'

'You're always fine to watch Jet play rugby . . .' Jade said.

'He's at a different level to you, honey. He's going to –'

'Oh, I know,' Jade interrupted him. 'He's going to play for the Wallabies. But what about me? I want to play for the Diamonds. Will you watch me then, or will you always be too busy?'

Jade saw the hurt look on Dad's face. She could see he felt terrible. Perhaps he didn't realise how much netball meant to her. Being focused on his business and Jet probably meant he didn't have time to think about anything else.

'Don't worry about it.' She stomped into her room, grabbed her netball and threw herself on the bed.

I hate arguing with Dad. But why can't he see how important netball is to me?

Chapter Seven

Jade woke hours later. She eyed the clock. It was after four.

'Oh my God!' Jade sat up. 'I totally crashed!' She hurried into the hallway.

'Where's the fire?' Jet said, laughing.

Jade laughed too. 'Haha. Very funny. I fell asleep. Are Mum and Dad home?'

'No, they've gone out for a jog.'

Jade frowned. 'They're always out.'

Jet steered her back into her bedroom. He sat her on the bed then plonked himself onto the red beanbag beneath the window, his long legs sticking out at odd angles.

It was hard to believe that Jet was only a few years older than Jade because he was so much bigger than her. Despite the size difference, they did look similar with the same green eyes and fair hair.

'Do you want to talk about it?' Jet asked.

Jade shrugged. 'Mum and Dad don't care about me.'

'That's not true,' Jet said. 'They love you. You're their little princess, remember?'

'It's been a long time since I played princesses,' Jade said. 'All they care about is their business. And your rugby. Dad never stops talking about you.'

'Trust me,' Jet reassured her. 'Mum and Dad may be preoccupied with work and staying fit, but they have our best interests at heart. They love both of us and they're always telling me how good you are at art.'

'But why don't they ever watch me play netball? I don't expect them to come to every game – just now and then.'

'Don't give up,' Jet said. 'Keep asking them. I'm sure they'll come if they can.'

'Okay.' Jade laced her fingers together in her lap.

'Is there something else?'

'I don't feel that I can trust my teammates. They're not as good as me.'

Jet laughed. 'What makes you think you're better than they are?'

'They drop passes. They miss goals.' Jade groaned. 'I know it sounds petty, but it's true. They make mistakes all the time.'

'And you don't?'

Jade considered her performance that

41

morning before mentally brushing it aside. 'Not really.'

Jet's eyebrows shot up. 'Maybe you're judging them too harshly. Isn't this your first year as a team?'

'Yeah.'

'Well, it takes a while for a team to work well together. You girls have loads of skills to master and if netball is anything like rugby, you're probably coming up against tough competition. But the bottom line is, you're on a *team*. As frustrating as it can get when people make mistakes, you can't play every position. You have to learn to trust the others and they have to learn to trust you.' With that, Jet jumped to his feet. 'I think I might go for a run, too. Do you want to come?'

Jade shook her head. She wanted some time to practise her skills to make sure she'd play better in the next game. 'I might go over some drills.'

'Have fun,' Jet said, before disappearing out the door.

Jade spent the next hour practising her shooting. She had a ring set up in their giant backyard, which was attached to the garage above the brick courtyard. She drew a chalk outline on the cement roughly the same size as the goal circle. Then she placed six of her mum's pot plants in an arc, so that they formed a curved line from the goal ring to the edge of the circle. The drill was called Shooting along a Curve.

First she started at the nearest pot plant and attempted to shoot a goal. When she was happy with her success rate at the first marker, Jade moved to the second marker and started shooting again. When she was happy shooting from the second marker, she moved to the third marker and so on until she'd reached the sixth marker.

Once she'd gone through all six markers, Jade adjusted the drill. She went back to the first pot plant and challenged herself to shoot from each marker in quick succession. If she missed a shot, she started again from the top.

Jade was having so much fun she didn't notice her parents and then Jet come home, or that it was getting dark.

'Jade, time for dinner!' Mum called from the back door.

'Coming!' Jade said, running inside.

Chapter Eight

The rest of the weekend dragged by, with Jade's parents working on Sunday. Jade was glad when Monday rolled around so that she had school to keep her occupied.

But then she remembered that today was her year's first surf awareness lesson. Jade had never surfed before and was very nervous.

What if I can't do it? Everyone will laugh at me.

Jade was already on the bus that would take them to the beach when she felt someone sit beside her.

'Isabella!' she gasped, surprised to see her Gems teammate. 'What are you doing here?'

'We're in the same year, silly! I'm doing the surf classes too.' Isabella grinned.

'Oh, good,' Jade said. She saw that Isabella was wearing an awesome red and yellow rashie with matching shorts. Her long hair was sun streaked and her skin was tanned. Jade, on the other hand, was wearing a tattered pair of board shorts over her black one-piece swimsuit. Her skin was pale to say the least.

I bet Isabella's a good surfer, Jade thought. *She sure looks the part.*

'Have you surfed before?' Isabella asked.

Jade chewed her lip. 'Um, yeah,' she said, not wanting to look like a newbie. 'Heaps of times.'

'Great,' Isabella said. 'I've been a few times with my dad and Maia, but I'm not very good. Have you ever done Nippers?'

'I don't need to do Nippers.' Jade tried to sound confident. 'I've been swimming in the surf since I was four.' Jade could feel herself sinking deeper and deeper into the hole she'd dug for herself. 'Hey, did you enjoy the game on Saturday?' she asked, trying to change the subject.

Isabella nodded. 'It was fun.'

'I know we lost,' Jade said, 'but we can still make it to the grand final. How do you reckon we'll go against Barton this week?'

'It's not going to be easy. We've lost one and drawn one against them.' She pulled a funny face then laughed. 'It could go either way.'

'Yeah, I think you're right.'

The girls spent the rest of the trip reliving the best games and plays of the season. Jade was amazed at how many details Isabella could recall. She practically remembered every goal any of the Gems ever shot!

'You really love playing for the Gems, don't you?' Jade said.

'Don't you?' Isabella asked. 'It's the best! Who's your favourite Diamonds player?'

'Definitely Erin Bell,' Jade said.

'I like her, too,' Isabella replied.

'Did you know she once shot 33 goals in one game during the Netball World Cup? She's one of our best long-range shooters ever!'

The bus jerked to a stop and Jade glanced out the window. She'd been so engrossed chatting about netball and Erin Bell, she hadn't realised they'd arrived at the beach.

I can't believe how much fun it is to talk to Isabella, she thought.

Isabella stood up. 'Are you coming?'

Jade laughed, gulping down her fears. 'Try to hold me back!' she said, as she followed Isabella into the throng.

Once they reached the sand, the surf instructor asked them to get into pairs.

Isabella turned to Jade. 'Shall we pair up?'

Jade was shocked. Isabella was popular and could have picked anyone, but she'd picked her!

'Sure,' Jade said.

'Now, I want one person to stand on the board, feet apart and arms out,' the instructor said. 'The other person is to get down at the back of the board and gently move it left and right to mimic the movements of a wave. The person standing on the board should work hard to maintain their balance. I'll come around and check everyone's stances.'

'You go first,' Isabella told Jade.

Jade stood on the board and pretended to surf while Isabella moved the board about.

'Hey, this is fun!' She crowed happily. 'I'm going to blitz surfing!'

Chapter Nine

'Jade, you're always so confident.' Isabella shook her head. 'I wish I was like you.'

'Really?'

'Yeah,' Isabella replied. 'You always believe in yourself. Like at netball. You believe in your netball abilities. And you back yourself to take tricky shots at goal. I'm glad you're on our team.'

'Even though . . .' Jade stopped herself just in time.

'Even though what?'

'You don't think I'm bossy?'

'Maybe just a little.' Isabella laughed as she held her finger and thumb a few centimetres apart.

'I just don't like losing,' Jade said.

'Well, no one really *wants* to lose, do they?'

'I'd never thought about it that way . . .' Jade said. 'My dad says that sport and life are all about winning.'

'Hmmm,' Isabella said thoughtfully. 'I like winning but I also play netball for fun. Even if we get knocked out this weekend, there will still be more netball. There's a summer competition coming up that we could enter, plus there's always next year. And no matter what else happens, we still finished second in the comp this season.'

'But . . . But what if there's a talent scout watching next week?' Jade asked. 'You know, like Lily's cousin, Eliza.'

'I'll just try to do my best. If I make a mistake, it's not the end of the world.'

'Everything okay, girls?' It was the surf instructor, interrupting their conversation.

'Yes, sir,' Jade and Isabella replied in unison.

'Well, it's time for a real surf.' The instructor pointed to the other kids heading towards the water. 'You buddies stick together, okay?'

Isabella flashed Jade a brilliant smile. 'Like glue.'

The girls bounded into the surf, cringing at the water's icy touch. Isabella seemed to know exactly what to do. If any big waves came their way, she duck-dived under them. Jade, meanwhile, struggled to keep afloat. Several times she was washed backwards and off her board, but she kept going.

When they were finally far enough out, the girls sat up on their boards and floated in the deeper water.

This is a long way out, Jade thought, peering into the water below. *I hope there aren't any sharks.*

Further out at sea, a huge wave started forming.

'Here I go!' Isabella cried.

Jade watched as Isabella paddled to catch the wave, then disappeared from sight.

Moments later she was back, glowing with happiness. 'Did you see that? I rode a wave! How awesome was that?'

'Pretty awesome,' Jade agreed.

'Your turn, now.' Isabella pointed to a new wave rolling in. 'Go, Jade!'

I have to show Isabella that I'm good at surfing, Jade thought. *And that I'm confident. She likes that.*

Jade paddled to catch the wave. She couldn't believe her luck when she managed to stand up but her excitement was short-lived. Seconds later, the wave crashed over her and sent her tumbling. Jade reached for the surface, kicking hard, before coming up spluttering and coughing, her hair bedraggled and her swimmers full of sand.

Jade was terrified. She never wanted to be tumbled around like that ever again.

That was scary! she thought.

Wanting to get out of the water as quickly as possible, she called to Isabella, 'I've had enough. You stick with Max and Lizzie. I'm going in.'

Isabella looked surprised but she didn't argue.

Just when we were getting to know each other, I've disappointed her, Jade thought.

Chapter Ten

Wednesday dawned cold and grey. Jade hated rainy days. It always made her think the sky was crying. And it meant she couldn't play netball at recess or lunch.

Jade dawdled over breakfast, not wanting to go to school, until Mum jangled her keys noisily. 'Finish up and go brush your teeth. I'll meet you out at the car. I've got an early appointment so we need to hurry.'

The rain seemed to bring Jade bad luck all day.

First, Jade's teacher, Mr Imble, gave the class a surprise geometry test. Jade hated geometry. Then, at lunchtime, Jade's lunch order didn't arrive so she had to traipse over to the tuckshop to investigate.

'There was a glitch in the computer system. Sorry,' Mrs McIntosh, the tuckshop lady, said. 'What would you like?'

'Tuna sushi, please.'

Mrs McIntosh checked the refrigerator. 'Sorry, we're all out.'

Jade groaned. 'Chicken sandwich?'

'Sorry. All gone.'

'Salad?' Jade said.

'Now that I can do.'

When Jade got her salad, she took it to the library. Stacks of kids were already there because of the rain. Jade spotted Isabella with three of her friends. She thought about saying hi, but the girls seemed deep in conversation. Besides, after Monday's surfing disaster, she wasn't sure Isabella would want to talk to her.

Half an hour before school ended, the clouds finally moved away, taking the rain with them. Jade was ecstatic. Today was their last chance to practise as a team before the preliminary final!

But when Jade arrived at the netball courts, she discovered she'd forgotten to pack her sneakers. She only had her clunky black school shoes to wear.

What if Janet won't let me train? Jade worried.

'Hi, Jade!' Lily waved, as she and her mum arrived.

Janet eyed Jade in her sports clothes and black school shoes. 'Where are your sneakers?'

'Mum forgot to pack them,' Jade said.

Janet shot her a quizzical look. 'Your mum forgot or you did?'

'Well, I forgot, but it's really Mum's fault,' Jade said, grouchily. 'She rushed me out of the house this morning.'

'You need to take responsibility for your gear,' Janet said. 'You're the one who plays, not your mum, and I bet she's got a million things to worry about besides your sneakers.'

'I know. I'm sorry, Janet.' Jade sighed. She hated getting in trouble. 'Do you want me to sit out?'

'No.' Janet smiled suddenly. 'Sorry. I've had a bad day. I don't know about you, but rain drives me crazy. You can train in your school shoes. That's okay.'

'Thanks,' Jade said.

Once again, she'd learnt something new about Janet: she hated rain.

Just like me, Jade thought.

'All right, girls,' Janet said. 'Warm-up time. Let's start with a light jog, then we'll do some stretches.'

The girls jogged around the court. Remembering how much fun she'd had talking to Isabella the other day, Jade slowed down to run alongside Maia.

'Hi, Maia,' she said. 'How was your day?'

'Um . . . okay.' Maia seemed wary.

Jade didn't know what to think. *Maybe Isabella told her that we've been doing surfing together. Maybe she's jealous because she surfs with Isabella, too.* Jade didn't want Maia to be uncomfortable around her, though. 'So what did you do today?'

'We had sport in the morning. We played netball at Marrang Indoor Sports Centre.'

Jade laughed in an attempt to put Maia at ease. 'That sounds way more fun than my geometry test.'

Maia groaned. 'I hate geometry!'

'Same.' Jade sensed Maia relaxing. 'Who did you play?'

'One of the other local schools. There were some girls from Greenfield who I recognised, plus others I haven't seen before.'

'Who won?'

Maia frowned. 'The score was really close, but I can't remember who came out on top. Hey, Prani,' she called to the girl jogging behind them. 'What was the final score today?'

Prani's eyes bulged. 'Can't talk right now,' she panted dramatically. 'I'm dying!'

Maia grinned at Prani's antics. 'We were all having such a great time we didn't take any notice. It was definitely more fun than geometry!'

Chapter Eleven

Janet stood in front of the girls and took them through a series of stretches, starting with their toes and finishing with their heads. Jade's favourite was the calf-muscle stretches. She got cramps after games if she didn't stretch properly, so it was nice to give her calves a warming stretch before training.

'Place your right foot out in front of you,' Janet instructed the girls. 'With your left foot behind you, press forward over your right foot to stretch your calf.' Janet pointed to the large muscle at the back of her lower right leg. 'You should feel it here. But don't stretch too hard or you'll injure yourself! Hold for ten seconds then swap to your left foot and stretch that calf for ten seconds.'

After they had stretched their calves and thigh muscles, they stretched their arms, shoulder muscles and necks.

'It's like giving yourself an all-over body massage,' Sienna said.

All the girls laughed.

'Great work.' Janet clapped. 'Shake your arms and legs out. Jump up and down a few times . . . Excellent. You're ready for your drills! We'll start with the passing drills you're familiar with.' Janet selected four balls from her sports bag and tossed them to the girls. 'Think quick!'

Maddy, Lily, Sienna and Isabella each caught a ball.

'Pair up. Start your passing drills,' Janet said.

To Jade's surprise, Lily and Isabella both turned to her. She couldn't believe it.

'It's okay,' Lily told Isabella. 'You go with Jade this time. I'll work with Prani.'

'Cool.' Isabella bounce passed to Jade. 'Are you still happy being my buddy?'

'Sure.' Jade grinned as she threw a firm chest pass back to Isabella.

The girls went through their passing drills until Janet called them over.

'After last week's game, I think we need to improve our teamwork and how we drive the ball to the ring. That means ensuring the Centre, Wing Attack and Goal Attack work together in the centre third and the goal third to deliver the ball to the Goal Shooter.

'We're going to go through what's called the Get it to the Shooters drill,' Janet explained.

She picked five girls for the drill: Maddy, Prani, Isabella, Jade and Phoebe.

Janet directed Isabella and Jade to stand in the goal circle while the other players were positioned further up the court.

'The attacking players – Maddy, Prani and Phoebe – start at the transverse line,' Janet explained. 'As they move towards the goal, they must pass the ball between one another five times before they reach the shooters, Isabella and Jade.'

'What passes do we use?' asked Prani.

'Mix it up to practise them all,' Janet said. 'But remember, each player has to move to a different position before calling for the ball, and you can't hold the ball longer than three seconds before you pass. Just like in a real game.

'The last attacking player to touch the ball should be on the edge of the circle before

66

passing to the shooters, who must also pass five times before trying for goal.'

'What about us?' Maia asked, indicating Sienna, Lily and herself.

'Until the first five players master the drill, you'll do a triangle passing drill,' Janet said. 'In a few minutes, I'll let you come in as defence players to make the drill more challenging. And don't worry, we'll change the groups around so everyone has a turn at different positions.'

The girls commenced their drill. Maddy, Phoebe and Prani brought the ball up court. After five passes, Prani was standing closest to the goal circle. She shot Jade a chest pass.

'Here!' Isabella called.

Jade sent a bounce pass to Isabella. The girls repositioned and passed until, on the fifth pass, Jade had the ball again.

Jade aimed for the goal, shot . . . and scored!

'Yay! I'm such a great shooter!'

As she tossed the ball to Phoebe to restart the drill, she noticed that the other girl appeared unhappy.

Maybe she's worried I'll take her position, Jade thought. *I definitely don't want to do that. Phoebe's an awesome Goal Shooter.*

Jade chewed her lip. Goal Shooter and Goal Attack had to work together in the goal circle, otherwise they would be overpowered by their defenders. Jade was convinced she and Phoebe would play better together if they got to know each other off court some way.

And she had just the plan to make this happen.

Chapter Twelve

Jade loved the new drill but she didn't get the chance to work with Phoebe in the goal circle because Janet kept changing their positions. Before Jade knew it, training was over and everyone was saying goodbye.

She searched for her mum's car but it wasn't in the carpark.

She's late again, Jade thought sadly, as she reached for her mobile.

Sorry, honey, running late. Can u make your own way home? Luv Mum.

Tears pricked Jade's eyes. She knew her mum loved her, but did she always have to be so busy? Water splashed on Jade's arm. She squinted up at the sky. Dark storm clouds were rolling in and lightning flashed in the distance.

'Everything okay?' Isabella said.

'My mum can't pick me up.' Jade smiled bravely. 'Luckily I live close by!'

'You can't walk home,' Isabella said. 'It's about to rain. We'll drive you.' She grabbed Jade's wrist and practically dragged her over to her mum.

'Can we give Jade a lift?'

'Of course,' Isabella's mum said. 'I'm always happy to drop our star Goal Attack home.' She winked.

Jade grinned, forgetting all about being upset with Mum. 'Thanks, Mrs Contesotto.'

Lightning flashed, closer this time.

Isabella screamed. 'Run!'

———

That night when Mum called Jade for dinner, Jade danced all the way to the kitchen. Her good mood continued throughout the meal as she chattered eagerly about the afternoon's training session.

'I haven't seen you this happy in ages,' Mum said. 'Has something exciting happened?'

'I think I've come up with a plan to help us in the grand final.' She reconsidered. 'That is, if we win this week's preliminary final . . .'

'What is it, Jadey?' Dad asked.

'I was hoping we could host a sleepover after Saturday's game so I can get to know our main Goal Shooter and the other Gems better.'

Jade popped a mouthful of her dad's delicious spaghetti bolognaise into her mouth. 'If we lose this week's game, we can practise our drills so that we improve for next season. But if we win, it would be a fun way to work on our team-building skills for the grand final.'

'How many girls are there on a netball team?' Jet asked.

'Eight.'

Jet winced. 'That's a lot of girls in one house.'

'It is, but it would be really useful for the team,' Jade said.

'I could stay at Brock's place so the girls can have the run of the house,' Jet suggested.

'Well, I think it's an excellent idea,' Dad said.

Jade shot Mum a pleading look. 'What do you think?'

'This means a lot to you, doesn't it?' Mum reached out to stroke Jade's hair, reminding her of when she was a little girl.

Jade nodded. 'I really want to get to know the girls better.'

'Okay, then,' Mum said.

'Thanks, Mum, thanks, Dad. You're awesome! But can we hold off texting all the parents until a bit later?' Jade wanted to run it by Isabella first to see if she liked the idea.

'Sure,' Mum said. 'Just let me know what you want to do.'

After dinner, Jade went to call Isabella to see what she thought about the sleepover. But for once, her confidence let her down.

What if she thinks I'm too needy? Jade thought. She glanced at the phone. Picked it up. Put it down again.

What am I thinking? Isabella isn't my friend.

Chapter Thirteen

'Okay, people, the waves are huge today so be extra careful and stick with your buddy,' the surf instructor said.

'Let's go!' Isabella tucked her board under her arm and jogged towards the water.

Jade followed reluctantly. Deep down she was scared, but she didn't want to admit it to anyone. The girls paddled a long way out then waited for a good wave to come along.

'That one's yours.' Isabella pointed to an approaching wave. 'Go Jade!'

Jade paddled for it but she couldn't get her rhythm right. She was floundering around so much her leg got tangled in the strap that kept her board close. The wave crashed over her, dragging her under. Salt water filled her nose and mouth. It tasted dreadful!

Jade kicked and splashed, weighed down by the board and tossed around by the motion of the sea until she felt a hand grab her and drag her out of the water.

'Hold on, Jade,' Isabella said. 'I've got you.'

Somehow Isabella got Jade onto her surfboard and back to the beach. Once there, she sat Jade gently down onto the sand so she could catch her breath.

'Are you okay?' the surf instructor asked, coming over.

'Yes.' Jade coughed and spluttered. 'I got dumped.'

'I saw that. Luckily your buddy was around to help you out.'

'It sure was.' Jade's cheeks felt hot and she knew she must be blushing. 'Thanks, Isabella.'

'No problem.' Isabella smiled. 'That's what friends are for, right?' She turned to the instructor. 'Is it okay if we sit here until Jade's feeling better?'

'Good idea,' the instructor said. 'Go back in when you're ready.'

Jade sat silently for a moment, staring out at the ocean.

'Isabella, I don't know how to say this,' she began, 'but sometimes I don't feel part of the Gems team. I feel . . . different.'

It was strange but oddly relieving to finally tell someone how she felt. She hoped she could trust Isabella.

'In what way?' Isabella asked.

'Everyone else gets on so well. You're always laughing and having a good time. Prani and Sienna are so funny and popular. And Maia, even though she's new, fits right in. I've found it hard making friends all year.'

Isabella seemed shocked. 'I can't believe you've waited all season to tell me! I never knew you felt that way. All the Gems think you're a great player. We love having you on the team.'

Isabella's kind words made Jade feel better. 'Thanks, Isabella.'

'Call me Izzy. All my friends do.'

A warm feeling spread through Jade, even though she was cold from the water. 'I also lied when I said I was good at surfing,' she confessed. 'I'm actually terrible at it.'

Isabella nodded. 'I know.'

'Why didn't you say anything?'

'I didn't want to make a big deal of it.'

'That was nice of you.' Jade took a deep breath. 'Are we really friends? Like you told the instructor?'

'Of course! Why wouldn't we be?'

'Well, you have Maia as a friend. And the other Gems. Plus you have plenty of friends at school. Why do you need me for a friend?'

Isabella blinked. 'Sometimes you say the weirdest things, Jade! I can be friends with lots of people. So can you.'

'And Maia won't mind if we hang out together?'

'No way! Maia's not like that at all. She's only been here for a little while, so she remembers how it feels not knowing anyone. I bet she'd hang out with both of us if she had the chance.'

'I hope so,' Jade said. 'The problem is, I haven't always been nice. I'm not good at making friends. I guess I'm just –'

'Competitive?' Isabella interrupted her. 'Focused? Determined?'

'All those things.' Jade sighed. 'I try too hard and I never admit when I make a mistake.

And I often say the wrong thing, even though I don't mean to. Nobody likes me.'

'That's not true. They just need a chance to get to know you.'

'I wish I could get to know Phoebe better. I think it would make a big difference in how we work together in the goal circle.'

'Phoebe can be very shy,' Isabella admitted.

'Well . . . I had an idea. I want to invite the Gems for a sleepover on Saturday so I can get to know them properly. I want to try to be a better teammate. What do you think?'

'That's a fantastic idea!' Isabella said. 'Count me in.'

Relief flooded through Jade. She was glad Isabella thought she was doing the right thing. 'Great!' Jade said. 'I'll ask Mum to send the invites when I get home.'

Isabella nodded towards the waves. 'Why don't we give surfing another try?'

Jade wanted to be brave but the thought of going back into the water terrified her. 'I'm not sure I can.'

'Don't worry,' Isabella said. 'I've got your back, buddy.'

Jade stood up. 'Okay. I trust you.'

Chapter Fourteen

'Mum! Guess what?' Jade burst into the house. 'I caught a wave. It was so much fun!'

'That's wonderful!' Olive said. She was bent over her computer, staring at the screen. 'Well done.'

'And I think I've made a new friend,' Jade said. 'It's Isabella from my netball team. She goes to my school, too. We're surfing buddies.'

'Is she the tall one with light brown hair?' Mum asked, turning to face Jade.

'No.' Jade shook her head. 'That's Phoebe. Isabella is my height and has brown eyes and long brown hair. She's very pretty. Oh, and she has three brothers.'

Mum frowned. 'I don't remember her.'

'Well, I spoke to Isabella about the sleep-over,' Jade said. 'She thinks it's a fantastic idea and she said she'll come. Can we text the netball parents now?'

'Of course. Let me see.' Olive scanned through the contacts on her mobile. 'Yep. I've got all the numbers here. What do you want to say?'

Together Jade and her mum wrote the invitation:

Your daughter is invited to a Gems team bonding sleepover at Jade's house. 15 Paradise Parade, Marrang, 2 pm Saturday. Ice-cream and scary movies included. Please pack a pillow, sleeping-bag and netball for some fun games. See you then!

'That looks good,' Jade said.

Mum pressed 'Send'.

Over the next few hours, Jade kept checking her mum's mobile to see if anyone had responded. Isabella's mum had replied immediately but nothing else came through all night.

'Don't worry,' Mum said. 'It's Friday night and some people might not be checking their messages.'

What if everyone's too busy or they don't want to spend time with me? This is my last chance to fit in with the team this year.

With a shock, Jade realised that she was as excited about just hanging out with the rest of the Gems as she was about the team-bonding exercises she'd thought up.

Jade went to bed early, intent on getting a good night's rest before tomorrow's game. At around midnight, however, she woke because of a nightmare she'd been having. The Gems had lost their preliminary final and had to watch while the other team celebrated. Everyone had been devastated.

Shaking her head to clear it, Jade slipped out from underneath the covers. *Maybe a warm milk will help settle me so I can go back to sleep.*

Jade was surprised to see a light on as she padded down the hallway. She found her dad seated at the kitchen table. His laptop was on and papers were scattered all around but he was fast asleep, his head resting on the table.

'Dad.' Jade shook him gently. 'Wake up.'

Dad sat up, gazing around with blurry eyes. A receipt was stuck to his cheek. Jade peeled it off his face, trying not to laugh.

'I must have fallen asleep,' Dad said. 'There are never enough hours in the day.' He raked his hand through his grey-peppered hair. 'What time is it?'

'It's past midnight.' Jade felt sorry for her dad. He worked so hard.

Dad gathered the papers together and tied them with a rubber band. 'I guess this will have to wait until tomorrow. Why are you up?'

'I had a nightmare that I lost my netball game tomorrow.'

'Is it a big game?'

'Don't you remember?' Jade said. 'It's the preliminary final.'

Dad nodded. 'That's right. Sorry. I'm still a bit sleepy. Now, you know that losing isn't an option, don't you?'

'I know, Dad, but sometimes it's not that simple.' Jade poured some milk into a mug then popped it in the microwave. She watched the milk spin on the turntable for a moment before speaking again. 'I don't suppose you can come and watch me play?'

The microwave beeped. Jade removed the hot milk and sipped it.

Dad yawned. 'I wish I could but one of my boot camp groups was cancelled during the week because of the rain so we're doing a make-up class tomorrow. It's worth a lot of money, so I can't say no.'

'That's okay. I understand,' Jade said. She wondered whether her dad might have more time for her – and for sleep – if he wasn't always so preoccupied with aiming for the top. 'But if we make it to the grand final next week, can you please try to come?'

'Sure thing. I'll see what I can do.'

Chapter Fifteen

Jade wiped the sweat from her eyes and tried to catch her breath. Despite the mid-week storms, the sun had come out burning hot for Saturday's game against Barton which, so far, had been fast and intense. Both teams wanted to win so badly!

Although Jade couldn't see the scoresheet while she was on court, she always kept track of the goals. The last one from Barton had levelled the game at 11–11.

Jade jogged to her starting position as Wing Attack behind the transverse line, waiting for Prani to make her centre pass.

Brrrp!

Jade charged forward. Prani passed the ball and Jade caught it safely in both hands. In an attempt to trick her Barton defender, Jade fake-passed to Maddy at Goal Attack, only to turn at the last second and pass back to Prani.

As the ball spun towards Prani, Jade realised her error. Her lob pass was slow, allowing one of the Barton defenders time to jump up and steal possession. Barton scored soon afterwards.

'Yes!' The Barton players high-fived each other.

12–11.

Jade was hot and frustrated. Wing Attack wasn't her favourite position and she'd been running around for the last two quarters without making much impact. It didn't help that the Barton defenders were so tall.

'If we're going to win, we'll need to score lots more goals. And quickly!' Jade said to anyone who would listen.

Brrrp! went the whistle, marking the start of the half-time break.

Jade stumbled off court and grabbed her water. She held the cool bottle to her cheeks, trying to take some of the heat out of them.

'Hang in there.' Mum hugged her. 'You're doing great.'

Janet called the girls around her. 'We knew this wasn't going to be easy. It is a preliminary final, after all, and only one team can go through to the grand final. But honestly, girls, you're doing a superb job and we're only a goal down. There is one strategy I'd like to see you using more, though. Anyone like to guess what it is?'

'Calling for the ball?' Maia asked.

'Precisely. In the heat of the game, it's not always easy to keep track of where every player is. You can only hold the ball for three seconds so make it easier for the player with possession by constantly finding gaps and calling for the ball. Stay one step ahead of your opposing player and let your teammates know when you're free. Got it?'

'Got it,' the girls said.

'Right. We'll switch positions for the next quarter to see if that helps, too.'

When Maddy handed Jade the Goal Attack bibs, her eyes lit up. Her dream position! She spotted Phoebe velcroing the Goal Shooter bibs onto her uniform and hurried over to her.

'Hey, Phoebe, I'm so glad I'm playing in the goal circle with you.'

Phoebe looked startled. 'I thought you preferred playing with Isabella. You did so well with her in the training drills.'

'Don't get me wrong,' Jade said, 'I *love* playing with Izzy and we're good friends. But you're our best Goal Shooter. And we desperately need you to shoot some goals today, otherwise we're never going to win!'

Phoebe smiled. 'Thanks, Jade. You're good at shooting goals, too, so we'll make a great team. You really like winning, don't you?'

Jade shrugged. 'I guess so. I know I'm a bit full-on sometimes.' She passed Phoebe the plastic container filled with quartered oranges. 'Want one?'

Phoebe reached for an orange. 'Sure. Thanks.'

'Jade,' Janet said, hurrying over. 'Remember that besides calling for the pass, you need to feed the ball to Phoebe. Work as a team in the circle.'

'Don't worry. We've got this,' Jade said.

Brrrp! The whistle sounded, calling for the girls to take their positions for the start of the third quarter.

The Barton Centre got a speedy pass off to her Wing Attack. Several minutes later, Barton were through the Marrang defence and at their goal circle. Jade sprinted up to the transverse line, stopping just before she stepped over it. As Goal Attack, she wasn't allowed to go in the Barton goal third so she had to watch and wait.

The Barton Goal Attack took a long shot at goal and missed. Sienna at Goal Defence scooped up the rebound and passed to Maia, who was now playing Centre.

Jade ran towards the Marrang goal, the Barton Goal Defence sticking to her. When she called for the ball, Lily threw a long pass to her. Jade dodged her opposition and collected the ball.

I may not be as tall as the Goal Defence, but I'm quicker!

Jade was still outside the goal circle so the rules didn't allow her to shoot.

'Here!' Phoebe shouted, darting around her defender to the middle of the goal circle.

Jade passed to Phoebe, who quickly went for goal.

The ball sank through the ring and the crowd cheered.

Calling for the ball and feeding it to the Shooter really does work, Jade thought.

Chapter Sixteen

It was the final quarter and the scores were still locked at 12–12. No matter how hard Jade and Phoebe tried, they couldn't get a decent shot at goal – the Barton defenders blocked them at every step.

Jade knew time was running out.

Prani, now at Wing Attack, intercepted the ball then passed to Jade. Jade did a super-pivot to turn away from her opponent for a clear pass to Lily at Centre. Calling and passing, the Marrang Gems had Barton scrambling to keep up for a change.

Jade flew into the goal circle, hands held high as Lily passed to her. She lined up the goal ring, her knees and elbows bent so that she could get maximum height when she shot for goal.

I can do this.

'I'm here, Jade!' Phoebe cried.

Jade hesitated. This might be her chance to shoot the winning goal. Imagine how good she would feel! Imagine what Mum and Dad might say!

But Jade knew she was taking a huge risk. She could see that it would be a selfish shot because Phoebe was better positioned, nearer to the ring.

Out of the corner of her eye, Jade spotted Isabella on the bench. She had her hands clasped together as she watched Jade anxiously.

Maybe I have to trust Phoebe with shooting, Jade thought, *just like I trusted Isabella with surfing*.

Jade bounce passed under her defender's long arms. Phoebe caught the ball and in one fluid motion bent her knees, lined up the ring and shot for goal.

The ball went straight in.

'Goal!'

The crowd cheered and clapped. Jade spotted Janet on the sideline, grinning madly as she gave Jade and Phoebe a thumbs up.

'Well done, Gems!' Janet yelled. 'Fantastic teamwork.'

Happiness washed over Jade. She'd done the right thing.

When the final whistle sounded moments later, the Gems hugged each other.

'You know what this means, don't you?' Isabella told Jade amid the laughter and chatter.

'We're in the grand final?' Jade replied.

'Exactly!'

'Isn't it exciting?' Prani said, flicking her long braid back over her shoulder. Her voice took on a serious tone. 'Ahem. Prani Patel, sports reporter, here.' She held her fist under Maddy's chin, pretending it was a microphone. 'Madison Browne, how does it feel knowing you'll be playing in your first ever grand final next week?'

'It's amazing!' Maddy gushed, going along with Prani's antics. 'The best feeling in the world.'

After a few more moments, the Gems collected themselves enough to congratulate the Barton team, before Janet called them over for debriefing.

'That was unbelievably tight,' Janet said, as the Gems formed a circle around her and the parents crowded in behind. 'I saw some excellent teamwork –' Janet's gaze rested on Jade '– and sharing of responsibilities and opportunities. Your special reward is that you're now in the grand final!'

Excitement rippled through the team.

'But we have to play Thomson again,' Jade said. 'How are we going to beat them?'

'There's no doubt that next week will be a tough game,' Janet agreed, 'but we've got all week to work on our skills and I know you girls won't give up without a fight! For now, enjoy the rest of your weekend. We'll regroup on Wednesday at training.'

What a great game, Jade thought. *I'm so glad Phoebe and I worked well together.*

Thinking about Phoebe reminded Jade about the sleepover. *No one has said anything about it yet. I wonder if they're coming . . .*

She leant close to Isabella and whispered, 'Has anyone mentioned the sleepover to you?'

Isabella shook her head then turned to the others. 'Hey, is everyone going to Jade's for the sleepover tonight? We can practise our drills there, too.'

Jade held her breath, waiting to see what people would say.

The Gems glanced at each other uncertainly.

'Um, yes,' Maia said. 'Is everyone else going?'

'I'm coming,' Lily said. 'My gear's all packed.'

'Me too,' Sienna said. 'I love sleepovers. Although I must warn you, I do snore.' She made a fake snoring sound.

'Why am I not surprised?' Isabella laughed.

After Prani and Maddy also said they were coming, Jade grew excited. That only left one person.

'What about you, Phoebe?' she asked.

Phoebe stared at her feet. 'I can't come.'

Oh no. She doesn't like me after all. I knew this was a bad idea.

Phoebe's dad put his arm around her shoulders. 'Phoebe's grandparents are visiting and we have a family dinner tonight.'

'Okay.' Jade nodded. At least it wasn't because Phoebe didn't want to come!

'But I can see how important this is to you all,' Phoebe's dad continued. 'Phoebe *has* spent a lot of time with her grandparents this week and you girls deserve to have some fun together . . . So she can come after all.'

Phoebe kissed her dad on the cheek. 'Thanks, Dad!'

'Yeah, thanks Mr Tadic!' Jade said. 'It wouldn't be a proper Gems sleepover if Phoebe wasn't there!'

Chapter Seventeen

'How much longer, Mum?' Jade said, peering out the front window.

'Relax,' Mum said. 'The girls will be here soon.'

Jade sighed and slumped onto the lounge. She'd never been good at waiting. 'What if they don't turn up?'

'They'll be here soon. Don't worry.'

Thankfully she didn't have to wait much longer for Isabella to arrive. She bounced into the house carrying a purple yoga mat, sleeping-bag and pillow. She also had a purple backpack with a photo of a pug on it.

Jade giggled. 'Hi, Izzy. I like your backpack.'

'And you're going to love what's in it.' Isabella unzipped the bag to allow Jade a sneak peek.

Jade's eyes bulged. The bag was brimming with packets of lollies, chocolates and chips.

'Quick, hide it before my mum bans it all!'

Isabella laughed as she zipped up the bag. 'Where are we sleeping?'

'We have a rumpus room at the other end of the house. We've got a data projector screen,' Jade said. 'You know, like at school. So we can watch movies.'

'Fantastic!' Isabella waved goodbye to her mum then followed Jade to the rumpus room.

'Is that where you're sleeping?' Isabella pointed to an inflatable mattress covered by a matching sleeping-bag. Both had a frangipani motif.

Jade nodded.

'Cool. I want to be next to you.' Isabella rolled out her mat and threw her sleeping-bag and pillow on it. 'That's my bed sorted.'

Jade couldn't help smiling. Having a friend was more fun than she'd thought it would be.

Speaking of which . . . Jade glanced at the clock on the wall, frowning. The tight knot in her stomach wouldn't go away.

'What's wrong?' Isabella asked.

'What if the others don't come?'

'Of course they'll come. And if they don't, we'll have the best night anyway because we'll get all the lollies!'

Jade nodded and gave a small smile. 'Good point.'

'I have something that might help pass the time until they get here.' Isabella reached into her bag and pulled out a netball.

'Awesome,' Jade said. 'There's a ring out the back. Come on.'

The girls played in the yard, taking turns at shooting. They started up close then moved back a step each time the ball went in. They lost themselves in the game until the sound of a car horn made them turn towards the street.

Jade spotted Janet's familiar car, out of which were spilling pillows, sleeping-bags and backpacks of various shapes, colours and sizes. Among the mess were Lily, Maia and Phoebe.

Jade and Isabella hurried down the side of the house to greet them.

'Sorry we're late,' Lily said. 'Phoebe took forever deciding what to pack.' She nudged the other girl playfully.

'And then I couldn't find my netball.' Phoebe held it up for the others to see. It was white with blue swirls and black diamonds. 'My grandparents bought it for me. I've been dying to show everyone.'

'Mine's better.' Sienna had just arrived with her dad. 'See?'

Phoebe looked confused. 'But they're exactly the same!'

'No, mine has "SIENNA" written on it.' Sienna laughed. 'So obviously it's better.'

Phoebe laughed, too.

Once Maddy and Prani arrived, Jade led the girls to the rumpus room.

'I have something for you all,' Sienna said.

The girls crowded around while Sienna sat down and rummaged through her overnight bag. She took out a brown paper bag and tipped the contents into her lap. Out came a tangle of yarn in the Marrang colours of royal blue, white and pink.

'What's that?' Prani asked.

Chapter Eighteen

'Everyone sit down,' Sienna said. 'We're going to make friendship bracelets.' She handed each girl strips of coloured yarn then showed them different ways to plait the colours together to make friendship bands. 'When we're done, we'll swap them so the band you make goes to someone else.'

In no time at all, the girls had each made a coloured band, which they swapped with a friend.

'This is for you,' Phoebe said, offering Jade the band she'd made.

'This is so cool!' Jade admired Phoebe's gift. Phoebe had used double the amount of white than blue and pink, which made the blue and pink stand out brightly. 'Thank you. I love it! Will you take the one I made?' She offered Phoebe the band she'd woven.

'Yes please!'

'It's so nice feeling part of a team *and* part of a group of friends,' Maia said, admiring the band Isabella gave her. 'When I moved here from New Zealand, I was worried I wouldn't make any friends. But now I have lots!'

I agree, Jade thought. *It feels good having friends.*

'We've got something fun to do, too.' Prani motioned to Maddy.

'Oh, yes.' With a cheeky grin, Maddy riffled through her overnight bag and pulled

109

out two plastic packets, one of which she tossed to Prani. The girls turned their backs and bent over as they fixed something yellow and orange on their heads.

They turned around.

Both were wearing chicken masks complete with bulging eyes, beaks and yellow feathers. They looked ridiculous.

'It's time for the Chicken Dance!' Prani declared.

Maddy pressed a button on her iPod, which she'd connected to a pair of portable speakers. The Chicken Dance music started. Maddy and Prani clucked, scratched and squawked their way through two verses of the dance while the other girls rolled around on the floor in fits of laughter.

Tears ran down Jade's cheeks and her tummy muscles ached. She'd never laughed so hard in all her life.

But a noise at the door stopped everyone in their tracks. Maddy stopped the music and she and Prani whipped off their masks. Several yellow feathers drifted to the floor.

'Hi, girls.' Jet waved as he sauntered in.

Stifling their cackles, the girls stared at Jet as if they'd never seen a boy before.

'Aren't you staying at Brock's?' Jade asked her brother.

'Yep.' Jet opened a cupboard. He took out a skateboard and helmet, which he held up. 'I was just looking for these. See you.' With a final wave, Jet strolled out.

Prani was the first to recover. 'Who *was* that?'

'My brother, Jet,' Jade said.

'Oh my God!' Maddy gasped. 'I can't believe he caught us doing the Chicken Dance!'

'Don't worry, he's not staying here tonight so he won't annoy us,' Jade said.

'Your brother can annoy us any time he likes,' Prani gushed, covering her mouth as she giggled. 'He's super-cute.'

The other girls erupted into another fit of cackles and squawks.

'How come we've never seen him before?' Maia asked.

'He plays rugby,' Jade said. 'Usually when netball is on. My dad goes to watch him play.'

'I wondered why I hadn't seen your dad much,' Phoebe said.

Jade nodded. 'Jet's really good at rugby. He might play for the Wallabies one day.'

'You're really good at netball, though,' Isabella said. 'The way you're going, you might end up playing for the Diamonds.'

'Thanks.' Jade shot Isabella a grateful look. 'Hey, wouldn't it be awesome if we all made it into the Diamonds one day?'

'That would be fantastic!' Lily said.

'Well, we are all Gems,' Sienna said dreamily. 'Little gems that might one day grow into big, beautiful diamonds!'

Chapter Nineteen

It was Wednesday afternoon. Training.

Janet put the girls through their warm-up exercises then called everyone over.

'Are we playing a game?' Maddy asked, as Janet handed out bibs.

'We sure are,' Janet said. 'And I have a surprise for you.'

Janet handed the Goal Attack bibs to Jade and the Goal Shooter bibs to Phoebe.

'Yay!' Jade cheered. 'We can work on our strategy for the weekend.'

'Precisely what I want you girls to do,' Janet said. 'This is our last training session so I want to make it count by putting you in your best and favourite positions. Sienna, you'll have to sit out at the start, but I'll swap you in shortly, okay?'

'Sure.' Sienna nodded. 'No problem.'

'Who are we playing?' Maddy asked.

'That's the surprise.' Janet blew her whistle. From the change rooms, eight other girls appeared.

'Oh my gosh, that's the Under 14s team!' Lily gasped.

'They haven't lost a game all season . . .' Sienna said.

'Make that the last *two* seasons,' Jade said. The Under 14s Marrang Opals were the envy of every young team in the area. They'd won their age group grand final the last two years and seemed set to win it again this season.

'They're so much better than us . . .' Prani said, looking nervous.

'Don't underestimate yourselves,' Janet said. 'Besides, you need strong competition so you can get some practice before the grand final. This will be good for you.'

The Opals girls said hello.

If this is what Under 14s look like, I've got some growing to do before next year! Jade thought.

Jade spotted Amber Flintoff, one of the star players for the Opals. Jade often saw Amber at the shops or the movies, but had never had the courage to speak to her.

'Hi, Jade.' Amber gave her a little wave.

Jade tried to hide her surprise. She hadn't realised that Amber knew her name.

'Hi, Amber,' Jade replied shyly.

'Right, girls, let's get started.' Janet tossed the ball to Prani, who was playing Centre.

The girls took their positions. Janet's whistle blew.

Prani passed to Maddy in Wing Attack, who shot the ball down court to Jade. Amber was the Opals' Goal Defence. She immediately put pressure on Jade, waving her arms to prevent a pass and shadowing her every move. Jade felt as though she were playing against the super-tall Barton team again – only the Opals were even better.

Amber had an incredibly long reach, which Jade struggled to get around. She tried bounce passing but the moment the netball was loose, Amber snatched it up and shot it away to the Opals' Wing Attack. Luckily for the Gems, the Wing Attack fumbled and dropped the ball. Lily, at Wing Defence, snatched it up, scanning around for support.

'Pass it to me!' Jade cried.

Lily threw a chest pass to Jade, who passed to Prani, who then passed to Maddy. After Jade positioned herself deeper inside the goal third, Maddy sent the ball back to her.

'Over here, Jade!' called Phoebe.

Jade pivoted and shot a lightning-fast bounce pass to Phoebe.

But when Phoebe shot for goal, the ball hit the ring and rebounded out of the goal circle. Amber scooped up the ball and sent it down court.

'Never mind,' Jade said. 'We'll get the ball back again.'

Phoebe shot Jade a look of gratitude. 'Thanks!'

As the girls watched, Prani intercepted a pass in the centre third.

'Go, Prani!' Jade said.

Prani winked before passing to Maddy, who then passed to Jade, who was running into the goal circle.

Jade eyed the goal ring then quickly checked everyone's positions. Phoebe was too close to the goal to shoot and her defender was towering over her. Maddy and Prani weren't having much luck evading their defenders, either.

'Shoot, Jade!' Phoebe said.

It was all the encouragement she needed.

Using a side step to get around Amber, Jade moved her weight onto her right foot and lifted her left foot off the ground. After checking her balance, Jade came up onto the ball of her right foot to generate power, then flicked the ball forward and pushed with her fingers. Amber lunged, her long arms reaching. The Opals' Goal Keeper jumped high, as did Phoebe. But somehow the ball made it over the defenders and dropped into the goal ring.

'She shoots! She scores!' Phoebe cheered.

'Great shot,' Amber said.

Jade's chest puffed with pride. 'Thanks.'

The Gems continued to try their best, but the final score was 17–10 to the Opals.

'Don't be disappointed by the score,' Amber told the Gems as they packed up. 'You made it really hard for us today. Good luck in your grand final!'

Chapter Twenty

Jade couldn't believe how quickly the week had flown by. It was Saturday already. Grand final day. Her tummy butterflies were performing loop the loops again.

She tied her rainbow-coloured shoelaces a third time then checked to make sure her Gems friendship band was secured around her ankle, under her sock.

'Breathe,' she told her reflection in the mirror, before she headed out to the kitchen.

Mum and Dad were at the table eating breakfast.

'Ah, here's our little champion.' Dad sipped his mango smoothie. 'All ready for your big game?'

'I sure am.' Jade tried to sound confident. She wanted to ask Dad if he would come to watch the game but she didn't want to push him. She knew he worked hard and still remembered how he'd fallen asleep at the table the other night.

I know he's busy. I'll still enjoy the game and do my best even if he isn't there.

Besides, nothing could spoil her good mood. Today was her big day.

'You need a healthy breakfast,' said Mum. 'What can I get you?'

Jade's stomach flipped at the thought of eating. 'I'm really not hungry.'

'You can't win a game on an empty stomach,'

Dad said. He handed her a banana from the fruit basket while Mum squeezed her some fresh orange juice.

Not wanting to disappoint her parents, Jade forced herself to eat and drink. Then she packed her water bottle and sunscreen and zipped up her bag. 'Mum, can you drop me off at the courts?'

Mum eyed the clock. 'It's hours before your game starts!'

'I know, but everyone else is meeting early. We want to watch the other teams play and go over our game plan.'

Dad put his arm around Jade's shoulders. 'You really take netball seriously, don't you?'

Jade laughed. 'I have been trying to tell you that all season! I've really enjoyed playing with the girls. I know I can be competitive –'

'I wonder where you get that from,' Mum joked.

'– But I've realised that everyone on the team is trying their best. And we're all good at different things.'

'As long as you shoot plenty of goals,' Dad said, as he pretended to shoot.

'I want that, too,' Jade said. 'That *is* the whole point of netball. But the Gems mean more to me than scoring goals. I love being part of a team. And I've made so many friends.'

'You sound like a walking advertisement for netball.' Mum laughed. 'You don't have to convince us. We know how important sport is.'

'Yes, but you're usually talking about individual fitness and performance and *winning*. I'm talking about the team as a whole, playing together and trusting each other. I thought I had to be the best player on the team but really what I want is to be part of a group of friends that has fun playing. And that's what the Marrang Gems do.'

Dad nodded thoughtfully. 'I hear you, Jadey. Sorry if I seem full-on at times.' He kissed Jade on the top of her head. 'Good luck today.'

Jade grinned. 'Thanks, Dad.'

Chapter Twenty-one

The game was not going well.

It was the third quarter and the score was 6–3 to Thomson.

Isabella took the centre throw and passed to Jade, who was playing in her favourite position, Goal Attack. She'd spent the first half playing Goal Shooter but she hadn't had any luck at goal. Phoebe had scored their only three goals.

Jade passed to Isabella, who then lobbed it to Maddy at Wing Attack. As Jade repositioned herself within the goal circle, Maddy returned the ball with a bounce pass, which barely made it through the solid Thomson defence. Phoebe was playing Goal Shooter but her defender was all over her. Jade decided to take a desperate long shot at goal, but she fumbled the ball. It bounced away and was picked up by the Thomson Goal Keeper.

'Grrr!' Jade growled.

'Never mind,' Isabella said. 'You'll nail it next time.'

Jade smiled. 'Thanks, Izzy.'

The Thomson team was keeping Maia super-busy at Wing Defence. Jade could see she was tiring. Sienna and Lily, the other Marrang defenders, also looked frazzled. Jade didn't know how much longer they could stop Thomson from scoring again.

Luckily, Maia intercepted a pass that was going to the Thomson Wing Attack. She bounce passed to Isabella, who sent a high lob pass to Jade in the goal third. Buffeted by the wind, the shot went wide. Jade raced to catch the ball, but her defender beat her to it, snatching it up with both hands.

'Never mind, Jadey! Try again.'

Jade searched the crowd. 'Dad? Dad!'

She couldn't believe he'd made it to her game after all! What a terrific surprise! If Jade could have run over and hugged him, she would have, but right then the ball came sailing towards the Thomson Wing Attack, who was standing right by her.

Here's an opportunity, Jade thought, as she leapt up to intercept the throw. She grabbed it out of the air before passing it to Maddy, who passed it on to Phoebe. Within moments, Phoebe had shot their fourth goal.

'Yay!' the Gems cheered, as the three-quarter whistle blew.

'This is where we get serious,' Janet said, as the girls huddled around her. 'Jade, you'll stay in Goal Attack. Keep working to break through the Thomson defence and feed the ball to Phoebe. Lily, you're moving to Centre and Isabella, you take Goal Defence. Maia, you're dead on your feet and need a rest. Prani you're back on at Wing Defence for the last quarter. Maddy and Sienna: you keep your positions.'

Jade glanced at Maia. Her cheeks were flushed, her hair was messy and she looked exhausted. Although everyone took turns on the bench, Jade would have been devastated if she'd had to sit out the last quarter of the grand final. Maia, however, seemed relieved.

'Short, quick passes,' Janet advised them.

'That's if we can get the ball,' Maddy said. 'Those Thomson girls are everywhere.'

'Everyone has a kryptonite,' Sienna said.

'What's kryptonite?' Phoebe asked.

'You know, Superman's one weakness: kryptonite,' Sienna explained. 'So what's Thomson's weakness?'

'They don't have a weakness,' Maia said. 'They're like the Opals. Super-tall.'

'So how do we combat tall?' Janet said.

'Keep the ball low?' Jade suggested.

'Correct,' Janet said. 'Use your best bounce passes and keep the ball low. And keep communicating!'

'Got it,' Jade said, then she raced over to Dad. 'You made it! Thanks, Dad!'

'When I realised how important netball is to you, I thought I'd better shuffle things around so that I could be here,' Dad said. 'From now on, I'm going to share my time evenly between rugby and netball. How does that sound?'

Jade smiled. 'That sounds awesome.'

'Good,' Dad said. 'You look great out there, Jadey.'

'Thanks, Dad.'

Jade spotted a familiar figure pushing through the crowd. 'Jet!' He was still in his rugby gear, which was covered in grass and dirt stains. 'What are you doing here?'

'I got here as soon as I could. I wanted to see you play in your first ever grand final.'

Jade beamed with happiness. 'You and Dad and Mum have made my day! How did you go at rugby?'

Jet shot her a lopsided grin. 'Ah, we got flogged.'

'Never mind. You can always aim for the top next time,' Jade said with a wink.

Brrrp! The whistle blew and Jade sped back on court.

Chapter Twenty-two

The Gems took the next centre pass. The Thomson players kept close to their Marrang opposition, making it almost impossible for them to move the ball into the goal third. Eventually, Lily got a pass to Maddy, who fired the ball to Jade in the goal circle. Phoebe and Jade dodged their defenders by repositioning and passing several times, before Phoebe could take a clear shot at goal.

The ball went neatly into the goal ring.

'Perfect shot, Phoebe!' Jade called.

6–5 to Thomson.

Thomson had the next centre pass. They quickly got the ball away to their attacking players. Immediately Prani ran in. She was like a terrier, badgering her opposition player and chasing her across court. When the Wing Attack dropped a pass, Prani scooped it up. Back up the court the ball came, all the way to the Marrang goal circle.

Jade shot for goal, but the ball hit the ring and rebounded.

Phoebe dodged her defender, collected the ball then shot for goal.

It popped through, and the crowd cheered.

One more goal to win!

It was Marrang's turn for the centre pass. Jade toed the transverse line, her mind and her heart racing. She could feel the tension between the players on the court.

The umpire's whistle blew.

Lily threw to Jade as she raced forward into the centre third. When Prani broke free from her defender, Jade shot a long, low bounce pass to her but the Thomson player reached it first, stealing possession.

The ball went back and forth between Thomson and Marrang as intercept followed intercept. Prani finally broke through with a high lob pass to Maddy. As Jade dashed inside the goal circle, Maddy bounce passed to her. Jade bent to grab the ball. So did the Thomson Goal Defence. The girls grappled for possession, neither willing to let go.

Brrrp!

'We'll have a toss-up, girls,' the umpire said.

Jade's hands were shaking. Her heart was beating wildly and she could practically hear the game clock ticking inside her head.

This might be our last chance to score, she thought.

Jade and the Thomson defender stood three feet apart, each facing her own goal end.

'Arms straight. Hands by your sides,' the umpire said. 'Hold your position.'

If I catch the ball, I'll feed it to Phoebe, Jade thought. *Just like Janet told me.*

The umpire held the netball just below Jade's shoulder height. Jade kept her eyes on the ball, her fingers twitching.

The umpire blew the whistle. The ball went up. Jade reached out, and beat her opponent by a millisecond!

I won the toss! Now, back to business.

'Jade!'

Jade pivoted on the spot, ready to pass to Phoebe, but Jade saw that Phoebe was stuck behind her defender. She couldn't break free.

'Shoot, Jade!' Maia shouted from the side-line. 'We've only got a few seconds left!'

Jade took a deep breath. 'You can do this,' she whispered. 'Be like Erin Bell.'

She focused on the ball and aimed for the ring, while the Thomson Goal Defence leant over her with her hands raised. Ignoring her defender, Jade lifted the ball above her head, aiming it towards the goal. As she flicked the ball forward, Jade straightened her elbows and knees, making sure she followed through with her hands to keep the ball on target.

The ball rolled around the top of the ring then dropped in.

Goal!

The crowd erupted and then, somewhere in the distance, Jade heard the whistle blow for the last time that season.

'We did it!' Isabella cried, as the Gems threw their arms around each other. 'We're the Under 13s champions!'

Jade saw the Thomson girls turn away, their shoulders slumped and heads hanging in defeat. One girl looked as though she might cry.

Jade was struck by how upset they looked. She imagined how she might have felt if the Gems had been in their position. *They've worked hard all season, too*, Jade thought.

'Hey, I have an idea.' She told the Gems girls what she wanted to do.

'We'll do it too,' Lily said.

Jade knelt down, untied her friendship bracelet and ran over to the Thomson Goal Defence, who had played so well against her.

'Hey,' she tapped the girl on the shoulder. 'What's your name?'

'Eve,' the girl said.

'Hi, Eve. I'm Jade.' She held up her friendship bracelet. 'I want to give you this. As a memento of our game.'

Eve's eyes lit up. 'These are your team colours. That's really nice of you.'

'You're welcome. You played well today.'

'Thanks,' Eve said. 'So did you.'

Jade glanced around the court and saw her teammates handing over their friendship bracelets and chatting with their opposing players.

'I think I've seen you before,' Eve said. 'Besides at netball, I mean. Do you live on Paradise Parade?'

Jade nodded.

'I live two blocks away. On Peace Avenue. Maybe you could come round one day and we could practise netball drills together?'

Jade smiled. It looked like netball had given her another friend. 'I'd like that,' she said.

'Team talk, Gems!' Janet waved the girls over.

As the girls hugged each other, their families and friends descended, camera flashes popping.

Even though Jade knew she wouldn't have minded too much if the Gems had lost the game, it was still an amazing feeling to win the grand final and to be part of such a wonderful team.

'Netball. Family. Friends.' Jade sighed happily. 'What more could a girl want?'

The Marrang Gems

Maia Anderson
Maddy Browne
Isabella Contesotto
Sienna Handley
Jade Mathison
Prani Patel
Lily Scott
Phoebe Tadic

Player Profile

Jade Mathison

Full name: Jade Astrid Mathison
Nickname: Jadey
Age: 12
Height: 149 cm
Family: Mum, Dad and 15-year-old brother Jet
School: St Thomas

Hobbies: Jade started NetSetGO when she was six years old and has been playing netball ever since. As part of a very active family, Jade has played many different sports, but netball is certainly her favourite. She loves practising goal shooting in her backyard, often using her mum's pot plants as markers. While playing for the Gems, Jade has learnt that netball isn't just about winning, that being part of a team and making your teammates your friends can mean more than scoring goals. Jade's closest friend is Isabella, who also goes to St Thomas. Isabella and Jade became friends while taking surfing lessons together. After initially being scared in the surf, Isabella taught Jade that surfing can be fun. All it takes is practice: just like netball! Jade also likes hanging out with Eve, who plays for Thomson. Eve and Jade have plans to practise netball drills together over the summer.

Netball club: Marrang Netball Club

Netball team: Marrang Gems, the Marrang Netball Club Under 13s team

Netball coach: Janet

Training day: Wednesday

Netball uniform: Royal blue netball dress with white side panels where 'Marrang' is written in pink. Jade likes to jazz up her uniform with her lucky rainbow-coloured shoelaces, which she reties exactly three times before each game in neat, double-knots.

Favourite netball position: Goal Attack

Netball idol: Australian Diamonds and Adelaide Thunderbirds player Erin Bell

Best netball moment: Shooting the winning goal for the Gems in the grand final against Thomson. Jade won a toss-up in the dying seconds of the match and had to really focus and believe in herself to score under pressure.

Netball ambition: To 'Aim, Shoot, Score!' like Erin Bell and one day play for the Diamonds – alongside the rest of her Gems teammates, of course!

Netball Drills

Shooting along a Curve

You can do this drill on a netball court, at the park, or anywhere there's a netball ring. Rather than practising shooting along a line going straight out from the goal ring to the tip of the goal circle, by following a curved line, you learn to shoot from many different positions in the circle. If you don't have a goal circle, you can draw one with chalk. Use six witch's hats or pebbles or anything else you can find as markers to create the curve.

1. Place six markers in an arc, or half-circle, so they form a curved line starting from directly in front of the goal ring and finishing at the edge of the circle.

2. Start at the nearest marker and work your way back to the furthest marker, taking a shot for goal at each one.

3. Take no more than three seconds at each goal attempt and count how many goals you manage to score.

HOT TIP

Try increasing the challenge by shooting from every marker in quick succession. If you miss a goal, go back to the first marker and start again.

Get it to the Shooters

This drill will help your team's attacking players learn to work closely with your shooting players. It requires five players: three attackers and two shooters.

1. Starting at the transverse line, the three attackers must pass the ball between one another five times as they reposition and travel towards the goal circle.
2. After five passes, the ball can be passed to one of the shooters.
3. The shooters must then move around the goal circle and pass the ball five times between them before they're allowed to shoot for goal.

HOT TIP

Increase the difficulty of this drill by adding a defender in both the goal third and goal circle.

One-foot Flamingo Shooting

This technique is good to use in the goal circle when trying to evade a defender leaning over you as you prepare to shoot for goal. Make sure you practise on a flat surface, so you don't roll your ankle!

1. Hold the ball in both hands, as if you were preparing to shoot.
2. Move your weight onto your right foot and lift your left foot off the ground.
3. Check your balance, then come up onto the ball of your right foot. This will help you to generate power behind your shot.
4. After aiming for the goal, flick the ball forward and push with your fingers, making sure you follow through.
5. Make sure you practise stepping to your left side, as well. If you practise both

sides, you'll be able to move either way to get around a tricky defender when you're trying to go for goal.

HOT TIP
Add in a defender to make this drill more difficult.

Netball Positions

Position	WA	GA	GS
Full title	Wing Attack	Goal Attack	Goal Shooter
Where the player can go	Centre third, your team's goal third but not the goal circle.	Centre third, your team's goal third and the goal circle.	Your team's goal third and the goal circle.
Player's role	To deliver the ball to the GA or GS.	To score goals and to help the GS score goals.	To score goals and to help the GA score goals.

C	WD	GD	GK
Centre	Wing Defence	Goal Defence	Goal Keeper
Everywhere but the goal circles.	Centre third, opposition's goal third but not the goal circle.	Centre third, opposition's goal third and the goal circle.	Opposition's goal third and the goal circle.
To deliver the centre pass. Plays an important role in both attacking and defending down the court.	To prevent the opposition's WA from getting the ball and to stop them passing it to the GA or GS.	To prevent the opposition's GA from getting the ball and to stop them from scoring a goal.	To prevent the opposition's GS from getting the ball and to stop them from scoring a goal.

OUT NOW

OUT NOW
Books 7 and 8 available July 2016